A greedy farmer lived in the same small village.
Hearing that the good farmer had gone to gather wood
and brought back a magic stick of plenty and become rich,
the greedy farmer became green with envy.
The next day he rushed to the mountain
with his A-frame on his back
to get himself a magic stick of plenty.

The Magic Stick of Plenty 2

Retold by Chong Cha-jun
Illustrated by Han Byong-ho
Translated by Lee Chunoc, John Harvey

The greedy farmer sat down idly under
the hazelnut tree and yawned and yawned.
Suddenly, "plock, plock, clicketty clack,"
a hazelnut fell to the ground and rolled
under his feet.
"Whoopee, a yummy tidbit," the greedy
farmer said. "I'll eat it!"
And he put it into his pocket.

"Plock, plock, clicketty clack,"
a second hazelnut fell at his feet.
"Whoopee, it looks delicious!"
the greedy farmer said.
"I'll eat this one too!"
And he put it into his pocket.

"Plock, plock, clicketty clack,"
and a third hazelnut fell down.
"Whoopee, goody!"
the greedy farmer said,
"I'll eat this one too!"
And he put it into his pocket.

Although the sun had not yet set,
the greedy farmer, humming to himself,
went to the abandoned cottage.
"Show up quickly, goblins!"
When the shadows of night fell,
goblin after goblin swarmed into the cottage.

They tapped the floor with the magic stick of plenty and cried,
"Come out, gold, tattoo tattoo!
"Come out, silver, tattoo tattoo!"
And out came dazzling yellow gold and glittering white silver.
If you tapped the ground with the magic stick of plenty,
whatever you named would appear.
The goblins danced around with delight.
Tittering and twittering, the greedy farmer stayed hidden.

In his glee, he bit into one of the hazelnuts.
It made a hissing sound,
"SSSSSSS!"
This startled the goblins.
"Oh me, oh my!" they cried,
"Whatever can this be?"
"Has that fellow come here again?"
"Let's get him! We'll give him what for!"

Very angry goblins grabbed the greedy farmer
from his hiding place.
"Spare me, please!" he cried, falling to his knees.
"I'm not that other fellow!"
But all the angry goblins said was,
"How shall we teach this guy a lesson?"

And the greedy farmer was beaten to a jelly.
"Help, help! I'm dying! I'm dying!" he screeched.
But the goblins all chortled,
"Flatten him like a flatfish, tattoo tattoo!
"Stretch him out like a snake, tattoo tattoo!"
And the goblins went on whacking the greedy farmer
with their magic stick of plenty.

At the crack of dawn, the goblins vanished.
Flat as a flatfish, stretched out thin as a snake,
the groggy, greedy farmer, dizzy and woozy,
stumbled back to his house.

"Come out, gold, tattoo tattoo!
"Come out, silver, tattoo tattoo!"
The good farmer tapped the ground
with the magic stick of plenty
and out came dazzling yellow gold
and glittering white silver. And then,
in a wink of an eye,
out came a fancy tiled-roof manor,
full of chests of gold and silver
and of other treasure!
The good farmer and his parents lived
happily ever after.

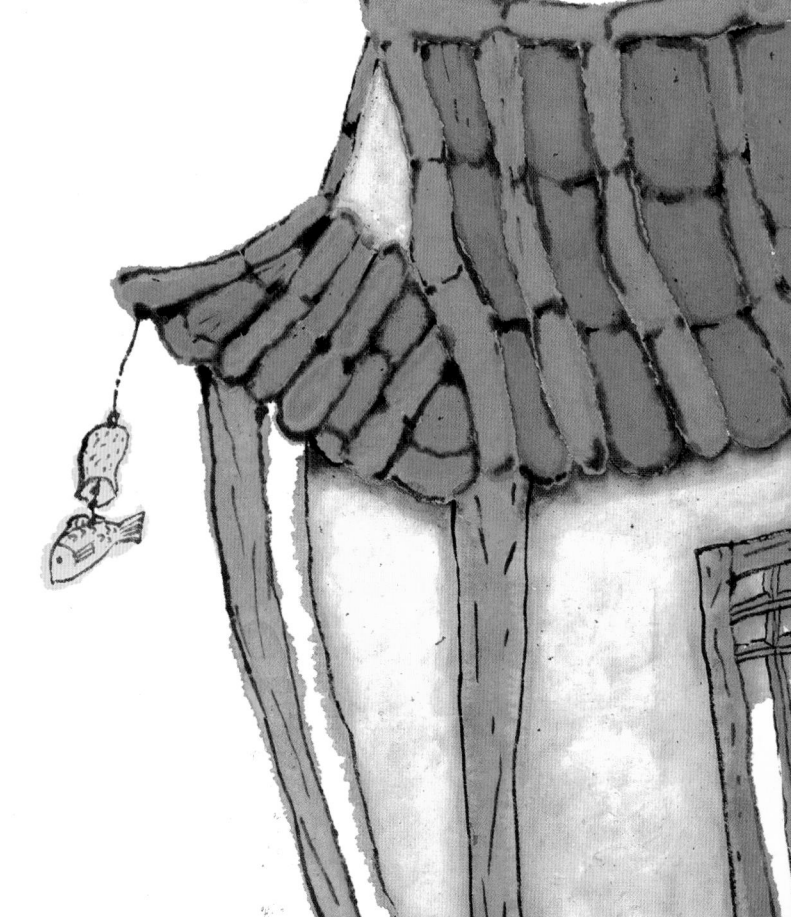

All the goblins scampered away
as fast as their legs would carry them,
leaving the magic stick of plenty
behind them on the cottage floor.
The good farmer took the magic stick of plenty
back home where his worried parents
sat waiting for him.

Quivering and shivering,
the good farmer
stayed hidden in a dark corner.
In his fear, he bit into one of the hazelnuts.
A loud sound broke like thunder, "CRACK!"
The good farmer was startled, and so were the goblins.
"Oh me, oh my! What is this?" they cried.
"Is the cottage falling down?"
"We will all be crushed to death! Let's get out of here!"

They tapped the floor
with their magic
stick of plenty
and cried,
"Come out, gold, tattoo tattoo!"
"Come out, silver, tattoo tattoo!"
And out came dazzling yellow gold
and glittering white silver.
If you tapped the ground
with the magic stick of plenty,
whatever you named would appear.
The goblins danced around with delight.

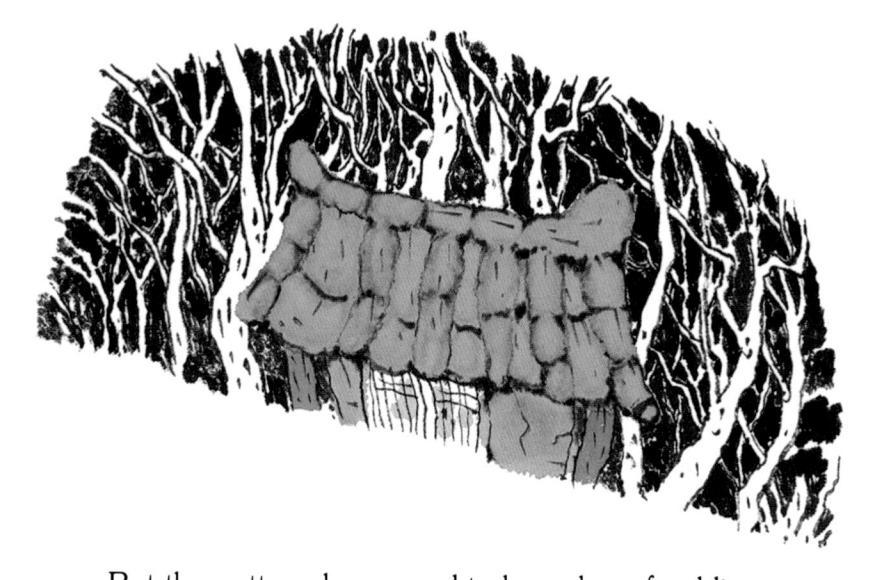

But the cottage happened to be a den of goblins.
Well, when the shadows of night fell,
goblin after goblin swarmed into the cottage.

The sun had set and it was growing dark.
"Where can I find shelter for the night?"
the good farmer asked himself.
He wandered about in the dark forest
until he came upon an abandoned cottage.
"Phew! How lucky for me!
I can sleep in this cottage,"
he said, and went right in.

"Plock, plock, clicketty clack,"
another hazelnut fell down.
"Whoopee! Goody!"
the good farmer cried,
"This one I'll keep for myself!"
And he put it into his pocket.

The good farmer worked steadily gathering
wood under a hazelnut tree.
Suddenly, "plock, plock, clicketty clack,"
a hazelnut fell to the ground
and rolled under his feet.
"Whoopee, a yummy tidbit!" the good farmer
cried, "I'll give this one to my mother!"
And he put it into his pocket.

"Plock, plock, clicketty clack,"
a second hazelnut fell at his feet.
"Whoopee! It looks delicious!"
the good farmer cried,
"I'll give this one to my father!"
And he put it into his pocket.

The Magic Stick of Plenty 1

Retold by Chong Cha-jun
Illustrated by Han Byong-ho
Translated by Lee Chunoc, John Harvey

Once upon a time, a good farmer lived in a small village.
The good farmer was poor
but took very good care of his old parents.
One day, he climbed the mountain
with his A-frame on his back
to gather wood.

Published by Borim Publishing Company

4th Floor, Keumsan Bldg, 364-22 Seogyo-dong, Mapo-gu, Seoul, Korea

Copyright © 1996 by Borim Publishing Company, Seoul, Korea

First published in Korea under the title '솔메 마을이'

English translation copyright © 1996 by Borim Publishing Company, Seoul, Korea

ISBN 89-433-0280-0

Printed in Korea